NICKELODEON

SpongeBob squarepants

HOORAY FOR DADS!

by Erica Pass
illustrated by The Artifact Group

SIMON SPOTLIGHT/NICKELODEON
New York   London   Toronto   Sydney

Stephen Hillenburg

Based on the TV series *SpongeBob SquarePants*® created by Stephen Hillenburg as seen on Nickelodeon®

SIMON SPOTLIGHT

An imprint of Simon & Schuster Children's Publishing Division
1230 Avenue of the Americas, New York, New York 10020

Manufactured in the United States of America
First Edition   10 9 8 7 6 5 4 3 2 1
ISBN-13: 978-1-4169-2782-2
ISBN-10: 1-4169-2782-4

"Hey, Gary, guess what?" said SpongeBob one morning. "Today's the annual Dad and Kid Games Day at Mussel Beach."

"Meow?" asked Gary.

"That's right, Gary," said SpongeBob. "It's a whole day for dads and their kids to play games and have fun together. And my dad's coming!"

When SpongeBob got to the beach almost all of Bikini Bottom was already there.

"I'm ready!" said SpongeBob. "Squidward, are you excited?"

"Oh, thrilled to bits," said Squidward.

"Patrick, are you excited?" asked SpongeBob.

"Yes," said Patrick. "I love the beach!"
"Mr. Krabs, are you excited?" SpongeBob asked.
"I'm excited to win the grand prize," said Mr. Krabs.

"Prize?" said SpongeBob. "You mean there's a prize besides the joy of spending the day with our dads?"

"Of course, SpongeBob," said Sandy. "This is a contest. Only one team can win the prize. But the prize is a surprise. No one knows what it is."

"Well, I hope it's a vacation to take me far, far away from here," Squidward said.

"I don't care about the prize," said SpongeBob. "I'm just excited to be with my dad."

Just then they heard *honk-honk!* A bus filled with everyone's dads arrived at the beach.

"Hooray for dads!" SpongeBob called out.

"Dad!" yelled SpongeBob. "It's so good to see you!"

"You, too, son," said SpongeBob's dad.

"Howdy, Sandy!" said Sandy's dad.

"Pappy! You look finer than a jackrabbit at a fancy dress ball," said Sandy.

"Oh, Pearl, isn't this exciting?" asked Mr. Krabs.

"Uh, yeah, sure, Dad," replied Pearl, looking bored. "I'm *so* excited."

"Hello, Squidward," said Squidward's dad. "At least it's not raining."

"Yeah," said Squidward.

"Sheldon," said Plankton's dad. "Isn't this a glorious day?"

Plankton turned red. "It would be more glorious if we won a certain secret recipe," he muttered.

"Patrick," said Patrick's dad. "The beach!"

"I know!" yelled Patrick. "I love the beach!"

"Gather around, everyone," said Kip Kelp, host of the event. "Welcome to our annual Dad and Kid Games Day. It's wonderful to see so many of our fine citizens out here for what's sure to be a great day, filled with teamwork and sportsmanship."

"Yeah, yeah, yeah," said Squidward. "Get to the good stuff."

"There will be many contests all day long," continued Kip, "and at the end we have a very special prize for the team that has won the most events."

"Did you hear that, Pearl?" Mr. Krabs asked his daughter. "That prize is ours."

"Just please don't embarrass me!" said Pearl.

The first competition was a relay race, which Sandy and her dad won.

"I knew I could count on you, Pappy!" said Sandy. "We're on our way to winning that prize!"

"Sandy," said SpongeBob, "there are more important things than winning."

"I think not," said Squidward.

Next was a competition to see which team could blow the most bubbles.

"Ha!" said Mr. Krabs. "My Pearl is an expert bubble-blower!"

Pearl sighed. "If I have to do this, I may as well win," she said.

SpongeBob and his dad blew beautiful bubbles, not caring about how many there were. Patrick and his dad went to look for buried treasure.

Squidward and his dad ended up blowing the most bubbles. "Prize, here I come!" he called out.

"Not so fast, Squid," said Sandy. "You haven't won the grand prize yet."

In the next contest teams had to build sand castles. Squidward hurried to build a really tall tower—but it came crashing down just before time was up.

"See?" Sandy said to Squidward. "You'd better calm down, or else that prize is mine!"

SpongeBob was all set for the jellyfish roundup. "Come on, Dad!" he said. "Jellyfish love me! And I love them!"

In no time SpongeBob and his dad had gathered the most jellyfish.

"Nice work, SpongeBob," said Sandy. "You just might win the grand prize!"

"Really?" asked SpongeBob.

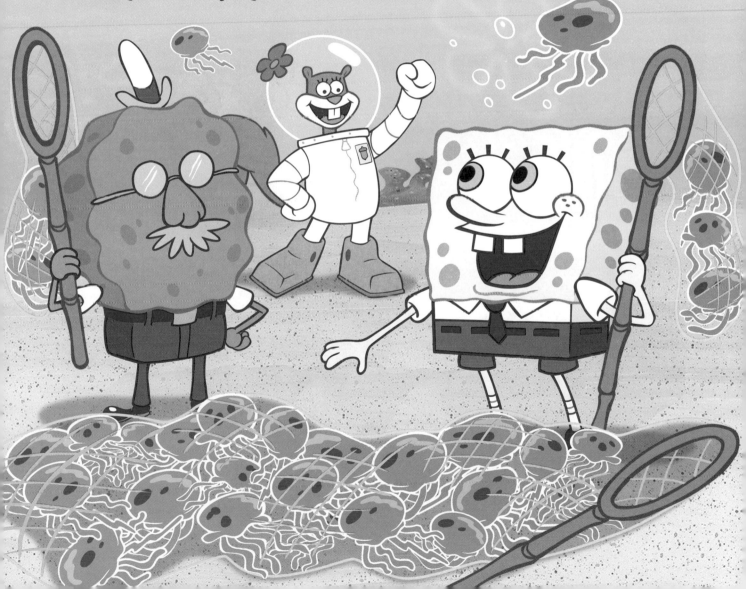

"Still don't care about that prize, SpongeBob?" asked Squidward. "I heard it's something you've been wanting for a while . . ."

"You heard it's a gold-plated spatula?" asked SpongeBob.

"Maybe," said Squidward.

"Oh, Dad," said SpongeBob. "I've been wanting a gold-plated spatula forever! We *have* to win now."

"But SpongeBob," said his dad. "I thought this day was all about spending time with the people you love."

"Right," said SpongeBob. "And I love spatulas. Let's go!"

The next competition was a badminton tournament, and SpongeBob did his best to try to win. He frantically ran circles around his dad, huffing and puffing and tripping in the sand.

"Out of my way!" SpongeBob yelled.

"You know, Son," said SpongeBob's dad, "there are more important things than winning."

"Of course there are," SpongeBob replied. "Like what I can do with that golden spatula! I can already feel it working its fry magic in my hand."

SpongeBob's dad sighed. "Oh, SpongeBob."

There were many more contests, and by the end of the day everyone was tired out—except Patrick and his dad, who had just woken up from a nap. They were in time to hear Kip Kelp announce the winner of the grand prize.

"This has been an inspiring Dad and Kid Games Day," said Kip. "I want to thank you all for coming out to compete. It truly shows the spirit—"

"Come on, already!" yelled Squidward. "Who won?"

"Okay," Kip said. "The winning team is . . . Plankton and his dad!"

Plankton hopped up onto the stage, excited. "What did we win?" he asked. "Is it the secret recipe?"

"No," said Kip, "you've won the honor of having your names inscribed on a plaque that will be placed in a new rock and coral garden in the center of town."

"Uh . . . that's it?" asked Plankton. "I ran around in circles all day long for this?"

Hearing Plankton's words, SpongeBob turned to his dad. "Oh, Dad, I'm sorry," he said. "I lost sight of what it means to be able to spend time with you."

"That's all right, SpongeBob," said his dad. "We all want to win sometimes. But you know what, I had a great time just being with you."

"Yeah, me too, Dad," said SpongeBob.

"Everyone is welcome to come to the Krusty Krab," Mr. Krabs announced.

"For free Krabby Patties?" asked Patrick.

"Never!" said Mr. Krabs. "But everyone can help themselves to as many napkins as they like."

"Woo-hoo!" said SpongeBob. "Dad, who needs a gold-plated spatula when I have you?"